Welcome to America, Champ!

✫ ✫ ✫ WRITTEN BY *Catherine Stier* AND ILLUSTRATED BY *Doris Ettlinger* ✫ ✫ ✫

Tales of the World *from* Sleeping Bear Press

ENGLAND

In memory of my English grandmother Gladys Vallance Beadle who, like the soldier brides, sailed across the Atlantic to America to be with the man she loved, my granddad Edmund Beadle.

—Catherine

To the Bush Brats, in memory of our grandmother, Mathilde Pangrazzi Bush

—Doris

Author Acknowledgment

A heartfelt thank-you to members of the WWII War Brides Association who fueled my enthusiasm and to the staff of the Queen Mary in Long Beach, California, who aided in my research.

Illustrator Acknowledgments

Many thanks to my models, especially John Young, Kyra Hissner, Jenna Colon, Adam Dickey, Bob Kubli, and Dave Young.

Sleeping Bear Press®
315 E. Eisenhower Parkway, Suite 200
Ann Arbor, MI 48108
www.sleepingbearpress.com

Printed and bound in the United States.

10 9 8 7 6 5 4 3 2 1

Library of Congress Cataloging-in-Publication Data

Stier, Catherine.
Welcome to America, Champ! / written by Catherine Stier ;
illustrated by Doris Ettlinger.
p. cm.
Summary: In 1945, when young Thomas, his mother, and his new baby brother leave war-torn England to join his stepfather, an American soldier named Jack, in Chicago, Thomas finds a way to give courage to a fellow traveler on the Queen Mary. Includes historical note about war brides.
ISBN 978-1-58536-606-4
[1. Emigration and immigration—Fiction. 2. Remarriage—Fiction.
3. Ocean travel—Fiction. 4. World War, 1939-1945—England—Fiction.
5. Great Britain—History—George VI, 1936-1952—Fiction.]
I. Ettlinger, Doris, ill. II. Title.
PZ7.S8556295Wel 2013
[E]—dc23   2012029990

There's been so much sadness in England since the war began. But on this day in 1944, we celebrate! Granddad walks Mum down the aisle. Jack Ricker waits at the altar. My British mother marries an American soldier. Now my mum is a soldier bride.

Mum's friends surprise her with a wedding cake
baked with saved-up sugar and powdered eggs. I take
my thin slice and find Jack.

"I have questions about America," I tell my new father.

"Okay, Thomas. Fire away, Champ," Jack says.

I write Jack's answers on scraps torn from a used envelope.

Mum and Jack have been married a month now, but Mum and I have lived with my grandparents since my father died. Jack stays at a nearby U.S. Army camp. Lots of American soldiers like Jack have come to England to train and fight alongside our soldiers.

Mum met Jack at a Red Cross dance. Jack taught Mum to jitterbug. Mum invited Jack to tea.

Now Jack visits when he can. He teaches me to play baseball with a broomstick. "Someday, Champ," he tells me, "we'll go see those Cubs play."

Someday means when the war is over. When Mum and I move to the United States with him. "I'm moving to America," I say out loud. I can't quite believe it yet.

I read the news of battles. Sometimes enemy planes fly overhead. Our village has been lucky. But London is hit hard—bombs even fell on Buckingham Palace, the royal family's home. The famous Big Ben, though, faithfully keeps time.

Both the king and our prime minister, Winston Churchill, have talked of service and sacrifice. My friend Miles and I help grow vegetables at our school's victory garden, since there's less food in the shops now.

Soon Jack must leave England with the U.S. Army. He's not with us when I become a big brother.

"Such a love," Mum says of baby Ronnie.

One spring day in 1945, church bells ring and Mum cries happy tears. "The war in Europe is over, Thomas," she says.

We learn Jack is safe but can't come to England. He's sent back to the United States with the other American soldiers. Mum and I must wait months to join him.

Mum reads Jack's letters. Ronnie learns to crawl. I go to school and play cricket with Miles.

When I come home from school one chilly afternoon, everyone is crying both happy and sad tears. Mum shows me a letter:

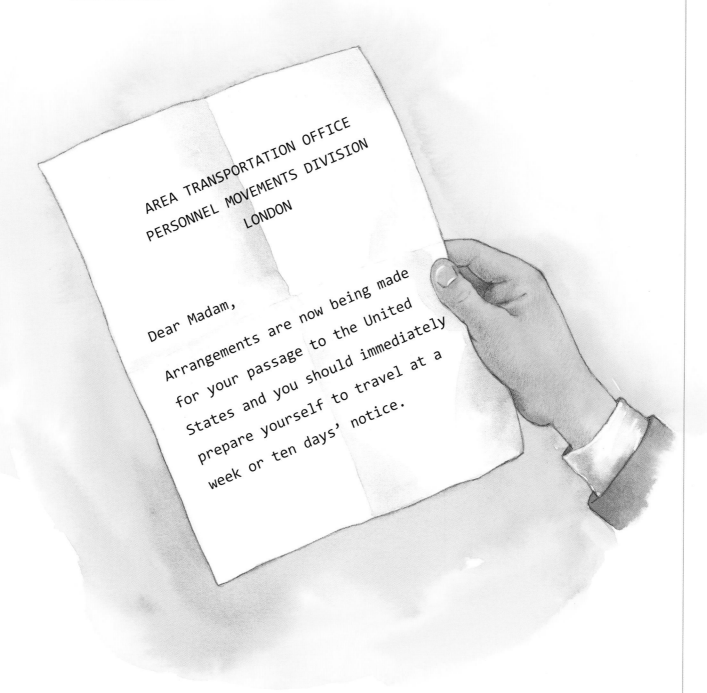

AREA TRANSPORTATION OFFICE
PERSONNEL MOVEMENTS DIVISION
LONDON

Dear Madam,

Arrangements are now being made for your passage to the United States and you should immediately prepare yourself to travel at a week or ten days' notice.

We'll travel to Tidworth Camp and stay with other soldier brides to prepare for our trip. Finally, we'll board a ship bound for New York.

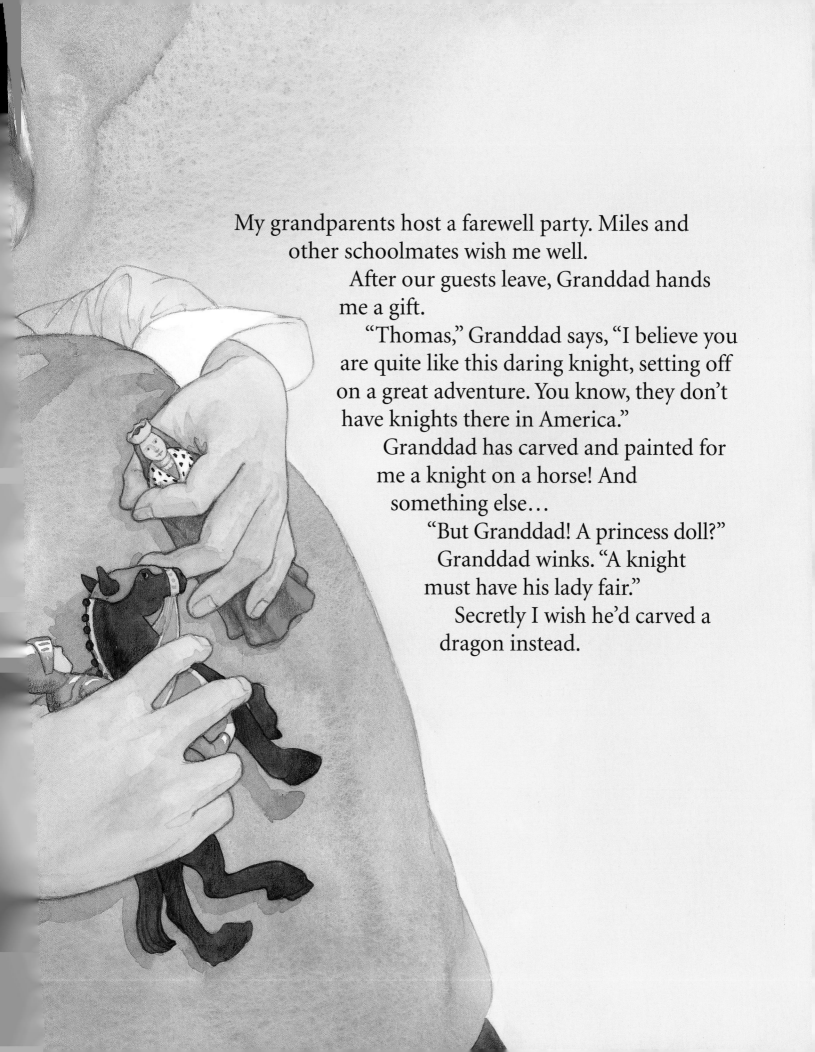

My grandparents host a farewell party. Miles and other schoolmates wish me well.

After our guests leave, Granddad hands me a gift.

"Thomas," Granddad says, "I believe you are quite like this daring knight, setting off on a great adventure. You know, they don't have knights there in America."

Granddad has carved and painted for me a knight on a horse! And something else…

"But Granddad! A princess doll?"

Granddad winks. "A knight must have his lady fair."

Secretly I wish he'd carved a dragon instead.

The next day we're off—
me, Mum, and Ronnie. From
the train I see a row of houses
with an empty space, like a
tooth gone from a smile. "A
bomb," I say, and Mum nods.

At Tidworth Camp clerks
check our papers, and doctors
check us. Soon, it is our
time to go.

Day 1. Depart England

When we arrive at port, I can't believe my eyes. It's the *Queen Mary*!

"Isn't she a beautiful ship?" Mum marvels.

A shout rings over the babies' wails and giggles: "Hey, soldier brides!" The man waves a camera. "Can we have a smile for the American magazines? Our readers want to see the happy British brides who married our servicemen. And those be-u-tiful babies, all coming to the U. S. of A.!"

Day 2. Day at Sea

It's early morning. I move quietly so as not to wake Mum or baby Ronnie or the four ladies who share our cabin.

I pull from my case the knight Granddad carved. I am not quite sure about this great adventure.

Later, Mum reads the day's activities from the *Wives Aweigh* news.

"Knitting class … baby beauty contest … or shall we go to story time?"

Story time is in the ship's playroom. There's a girl, Lucy, about my age.

"I'll tell you something," a Red Cross worker says to Lucy and me, over the noise. "Princess Elizabeth and Princess Margaret Rose once slid down that very slide." Lucy's eyes grow wide. "The English princesses!" she cries.

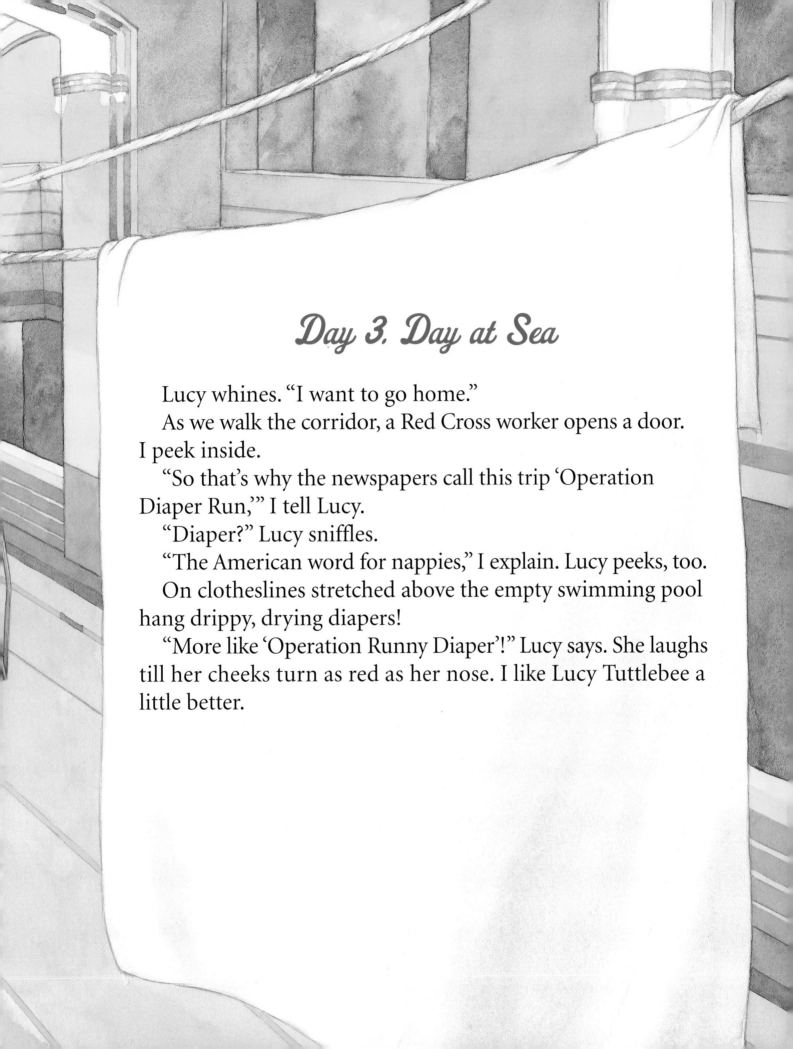

Day 3. Day at Sea

Lucy whines. "I want to go home."

As we walk the corridor, a Red Cross worker opens a door. I peek inside.

"So that's why the newspapers call this trip 'Operation Diaper Run,'" I tell Lucy.

"Diaper?" Lucy sniffles.

"The American word for nappies," I explain. Lucy peeks, too.

On clotheslines stretched above the empty swimming pool hang drippy, drying diapers!

"More like 'Operation Runny Diaper'!" Lucy says. She laughs till her cheeks turn as red as her nose. I like Lucy Tuttlebee a little better.

Day 4. Day at Sea

I clutch slips of paper. Each scrap holds an answer to a question I had asked Jack. I unwind one scrap. Maple Street. That's where I'll live with Mum and Ronnie and Jack. Another is a town, Chicago. But the name I wonder and worry about most isn't a street or town. I open my most crumpled scrap. Kingsley Grade School. I think about that school a lot.

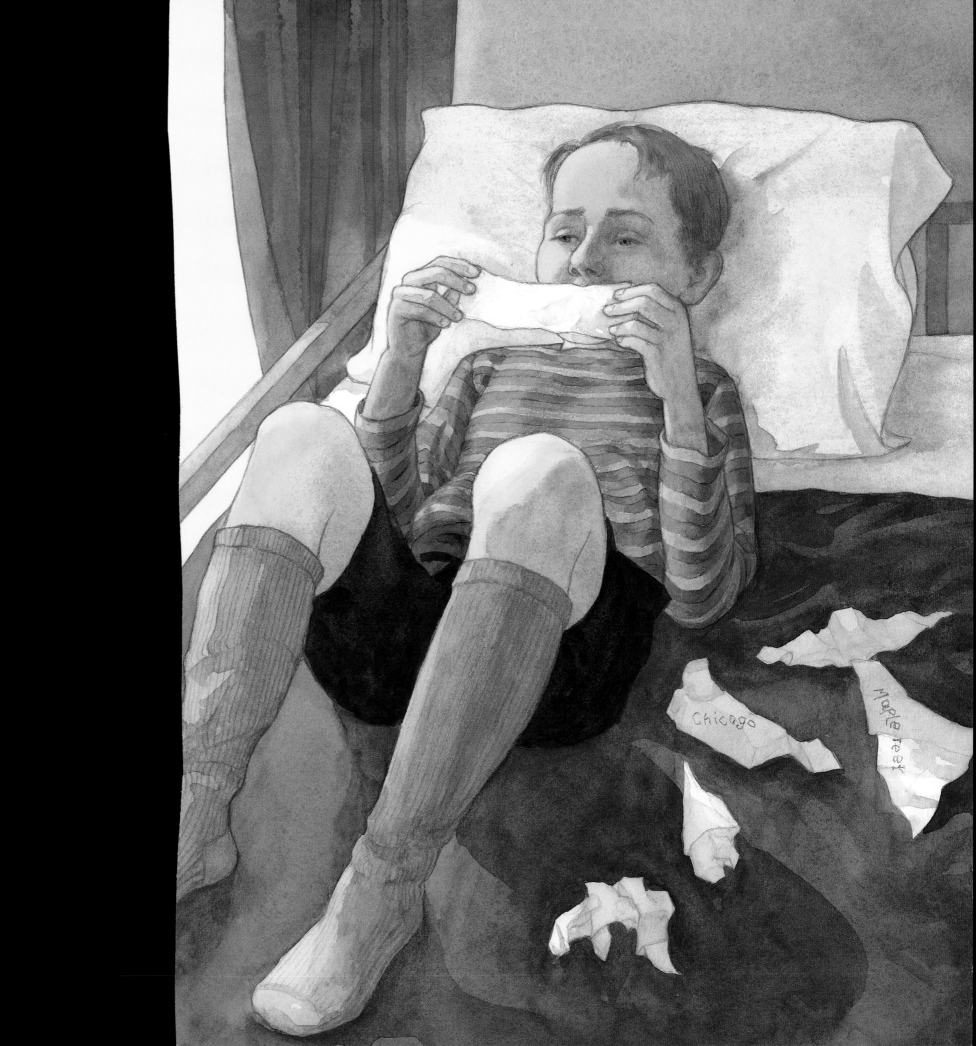

Day 5. Arrive United States

Rap, rap, rap.

It is very early. Mum rushes to the door.

"It's time," I hear. "You can see her now!"

"Quickly, Thomas, wrap up in your blanket!" my mother says.

"I'll stay here with Ronnie," Mum says. "Now go with Mrs. Tuttlebee and Lucy!"

I run with Lucy and her mother down the corridor. On the outside deck, a group has gathered. Someone sings, very softly, "God Bless America."

"There," says Mrs. Tuttlebee. "Get a look."

In the distance, I see a glow.

"It's her," says Mrs. Tuttlebee. "It's Lady Liberty."

"The Statue of Liberty!" I say. Lucy begins to cry.

Mrs. Tuttlebee pats Lucy. "Still a bit homesick, child?" she asks Lucy.

The proud, crowned symbol of America makes me think of another lady with a crown—and a way to help my friend.

"May I walk with Lucy?" I ask. "My mum is at our cabin. We'll head there."

Mrs. Tuttlebee nods.

At our cabin, I pull out my case.

"Lucy," I whisper, recalling Granddad's words. "I believe you are quite like this English princess, setting off on a great adventure. You know, they don't have princesses in America."

I hand Lucy the figure. I am glad, now, that it's not a dragon.

"Oh," says Lucy. "To keep?"

I know Granddad wouldn't mind. "To keep," I say.

"Thank you, Thomas," says Lucy. "I'll try to be brave, like you."

Brave. I am a little brave. Perhaps I am just a bit like a daring English knight.